Snuggle Pup

A Book About Feelings

Written by Marisa Johnston
and Christian Lester

Illustrated by Christian Lester

Snuggle Pup

Published by Marisa Johnston
ISBN 978-0-578-30508-0 (hardback)

Illustrated by Christian Lester

Printed in the USA

This book is dedicated to
my dad, Steve Cusenza.
To living life to the
fullest and watching
more sunsets!
-MJ

This book is dedicated
to my dog, Oreo, who
has given me many
ideas to write about.
She may be small, but
she is fearless, and I
wouldn't be the
author I am today
without her.
-CL

Meet Snuggle Pup, also known as Snuggy. This soft, cute fur-ball has feelings just the same as you and me. Snuggy had never learned how to let himself feel all of his feelings. Snuggy thought he should ALWAYS feel happy. Until one day . . . everything changed.

As Snuggy was walking in his neighborhood,
a boy dropped his ice cream cone and began to cry.

The boy kept crying until he felt better. Snuggy was puzzled. He had never cried like that and always tried not to feel sad. If he ever began to feel sad, he pretended the feeling was not happening. Next time he felt sad, maybe all he needed to do was cry.

As Snuggy thought about this, a garbage truck zoomed by. Snuggy felt scared.

He didn't want anyone to know he felt scared, so he ran away as fast as he could. He tried to talk himself out of feeling scared.

Next, Snuggy ran to the neighborhood dog park. He joined in on the fun with his friends. Then a Chihuahua handed out birthday invitations to everyone but him. This made Snuggy feel sad, left out, and not good about himself.

Hours later, Snuggy noticed that even though he was alone, his feelings were still with him. Tears ran down his face and he realized that they were helping him to feel better. Snuggy allowed himself to cry freely until he felt lightness inside him.

Snuggy went out of his
doghouse, ready to face
the world of comfortable
and uncomfortable
feelings.

Snuggy peeked through his neighbor's window and saw that she was making his favorite, chocolate chip cookies. All of a sudden he was faced with another uncomfortable feeling . . . jealousy! He wished so badly that he could join his neighbor.

At that moment, everything changed. Snuggy did something braver than he had ever done before. He let himself feel the uncomfortable feeling of jealousy and asked, "What do I need right now to help me feel better? How can I let myself feel these feelings?"

Snuggy put on an apron and joined in. His neighbor said that she was baking because she needed a break. She had been angry at her brother for stealing her beach ball. Snuggy was impressed that she took a break when she felt angry, instead of making a choice that would only make things worse.

Snuggy asked the girl what else she did when she had uncomfortable feelings.

On Snuggy's way home,
he felt something squishy
under his paw and smelled
a horrible scent.

He had stepped in dog poo! He felt
frustrated. Instead of punching
a tree, he paused and took some
deep breaths. This made both him
and the tree feel much better.

After cleaning his paw, he
continued to walk home, thinking
about what he'd learned that
afternoon. Snuggy realized
that instead of pretending
uncomfortable feelings don't
happen, all you have to do is give
yourself time and space to feel
them. Then they will pass.

Snuggy looked up at the clouds in the sky. He thought, Clouds come and go and are always changing. Feelings are like that too.

As Snuggy sat on the grass and watched the sunset, he realized some days are cloudy and some are clear. But no matter what kind of day it is, the weather will change again. Snuggy felt calm, thinking about this day that changed his life forever.

Meet The Authors!

Christian Lester (age 10), kid author and illustrator, demonstrated creativity and talent at a young age. He started drawing and telling stories when he was in preschool. With the support of his parents, he created books, sold art at lemonade stands, amazed his teachers and inspired his classmates. He wants to be an author when he grows up and hopes to inspire other kids to follow their dreams.

Marisa Johnston has been a teacher for 13 years. She is passionate about children's well-being and finding each child's strength. When Christian entered her classroom years ago, she looked forward to the day he published his first book. Years later, she came up with the idea of Snuggle Pup. At that moment, she knew just who her illustrator and co-author would be . . . Christian!

CPSIA information can be obtained
at www.ICGtesting.com
Printed in the USA
BVHW021911200422
634878BV00006B/29